Other titles in this series:
Barnaby's Cuckoo Clock
Flipperty's Aeroplane
Tufty's Pot of Paint

ISBN 0-86163-232-X

Copyright © 1988 Award Publications Limited
First published 1988
Fourth impression 1994

Published by Award Publications Limited,
1st Floor, Goodyear House,
52-56 Osnaburgh Street, London NW1 3NS

Printed in Singapore

LARRY'S
CARAVAN

Written and illustrated
by
Rene Cloke

AWARD PUBLICATIONS

LONDON

Larry, the puppy from Hopping Wood Farm sat on the step of his caravan and told Dumpling, the piglet, and Merry, the kitten, about his plans.

"I am going for a holiday in my caravan," he said, "I shall be away for a week and I expect I shall spend most of the time camping in Hopping Wood by the river."

Merry washed her face carefully.

"Too wet," she said.

"Have you any room for me?" asked Dumpling, "I've never been in a caravan."

Larry laughed.

"Not this time," he said, "my friend Tatters is going with me; I shall pick him up at the crossroads. Now let me see if I have everything I shall want."

He looked inside the caravan.

"A saucepan, a kettle and a frying pan. Three bags of biscuits, a bag of bones, some tins of meat and four tins of milk; straw and blankets. We shall be very cosy."

There were two little bunks just big enough for the two puppies.

Larry took everything out and packed it all in again to be quite sure he had not forgotten anything.

It was getting late by the
time he was ready and then there
were more delays. Harriet Hen
came running up with a basket of
eggs.

Then two ducklings had to
be chased out of the caravan
where they had been hiding.

"Quack! quack!"they cried. "We *did* want to go
for a holiday! A week by the river would have been
splendid!"

Larry hooked the caravan to his little car.

"Goodbye! goodbye!" he barked, "I must be off!"

"Goodbye!" cried all the other animals. "Have a good holiday and don't forget to meet Tatters!"

Off went Larry, the caravan bumping out of the farmyard and down the lane.

Everything banged and clattered in a most exciting way and rabbits and squirrels popped out to see what was happening.

The moon had risen and Oscar Owl swooped
softly overhead.

"Tu-whit who-who's making all this noise?" he
hooted, but he did not stop to find out.

Larry went bumping along. "I hope Tatters won't be tired of waiting," he murmured to himself, "ah, there he is!"

Larry could just see a little figure waiting at the signpost as he rattled to a standstill.

"Sorry to be late," he called out, "just jump in and choose yourself a bunk. I'm making for the river bank – it will be a good camping place."

　　The little figure waved a paw and hopped up
the step of the caravan carrying his bundle on
a stick over his shoulder.
　　Larry plunged forward and off they went
along the path through Hopping Wood.

When they reached the riverside, Larry
crept from his car to the caravan.

"Tatters must be asleep," he decided as he
listened to the faint snores, "I won't wake him,"
and he climbed up into the other bunk.

He rolled himself in his blanket and was soon
fast asleep.

Larry awoke early the next morning and got breakfast ready on the river bank; then he peeped into the caravan.

He had a big surprise.

The puppy who rolled out of the blanket was not Tatters after all!

"How did you get there?" asked Larry. "And what's your name?"

"I'm Rags and I was running away from Hilltop Farm," explained the strange puppy. "When you came along I was very glad to have a lift."

"But why are you running away?" asked Larry.

"I have four brothers and sisters," said Rags, "and the kennel is very full. My mummy said she had found a good home for me at Hopping Wood Farm but I didn't want to go."

"Hopping Wood Farm!" cried Larry. "Why, that's where I live. Oh, you'll be very happy there!"

Rags cheered up when he heard this and both puppies settled down to breakfast on the grassy bank by the river.

It was a lovely morning.

The biscuits and milk tasted very good and they each had one of Harriet's eggs.

But where was Larry's friend Tatters?

Tatters had arrived at the crossroads even later than Larry.

He had spent all day packing and had to carry a heavy basket of food as well as his bag.

He sat on a stone and waited for a very long time.

"Oh dear!" he sighed at last. "Larry must have got tired of waiting and gone on without me."

So he picked up his luggage and decided to find his way to Hopping Wood Farm.

"Someone may be able to tell me where Larry is going to camp," he thought.

But it was very dark and poor Tatters lost his way.

He tried to take a short cut through the wood but the roots of the trees tripped him up, the brambles caught at his coat and he nearly lost his basket of food in a pond.

At last, as the sun came up he reached
a big oak-tree where the rabbits and squirrels
were waking up and opening their doors.

He stopped in front of the little shop where Barnaby Bunny was taking down the shutters and Bertha was cleaning the doorstep.

"Hullo," said Barnaby, "you look as though you have come a long way."

"Oh, I have!" sighed Tatters. "I've been walking all night. I lost my way in the wood and I don't know where I am."

"Sit down and have some breakfast," said Bertha Bunny, "and we will see if we can help you."

Tatters was too big to get comfortably into the rabbits' shop so Barnaby and Bertha brought out bowls of porridge and some bread and butter, marmalade and tea.

"This is good," said Tatters, as he
lapped up the porridge.

By the time he had finished his
breakfast he was feeling much better
and ready to start looking for the
caravan again.

"Can you tell me the way to Hopping Wood Farm?" he asked the rabbits. "My friend Larry lives there and we are going for a holiday together in his caravan."

"You must go through the wood and along the lane," said Barnaby, "but you won't find Larry. He started last night and passed me in his caravan, rattling and banging along – I had to jump into the hedge out of his way."

"He will have gone a long way by now," moaned Tatters.

"I have a good idea!" cried Bertha. "We'll ask Tufty Squirrel to row you down the river until you find the caravan."

So they hurried down to the river where Tufty kept his boat.

"This is the first time I've been in a boat," said Tatters.

He was rather heavy for the little boat but Tufty managed to row along and at last they saw the caravan resting on the river bank.

Larry and Rags were bathing in the river.

"Hullo! hullo!" they shouted. "Come and join us!"

The three puppies had a lovely holiday and Rags was quite happy to go and live at Hopping Wood Farm with Larry.